Nipper McFee

ouble with **Mrs Lulu Lamb**

For Matthew
R.I.

For Milly
M.W.

Reading Consultant: Prue Goodwin, Lecturer in literacy and children's books

ORCHARD BOOKS
338 Euston Road, London NW1 3BH
Orchard Books Australia
Hachette Children's Books
Level 17/207 Kent Street, Sydney NSW 2000

First published in 2010 by Orchard Books
First paperback publication in 2011

Text © Rose Impey 2010
Illustrations © Melanie Williamson 2010

A CIP catalogue record for this book is available from the British Library.

ISBN 978 1 40830 219 4 (hardback)
ISBN 978 1 40830 227 9 (paperback)

1 3 5 7 9 10 8 6 4 2 (hardback)
1 3 5 7 9 10 8 6 4 2 (paperback)
Printed in China

Orchard Books is a division of Hachette Children's Books,
an Hachette UK company.

www.hachette.co.uk

In Trouble with **Mrs Lulu Lamb**

Written by ROSE IMPEY

Illustrated by MELANIE WILLIAMSON

ORCHARD BOOKS

Nipper McFee was often in trouble
with the neighbours . . .

Especially Mrs Lulu Lamb,
who lived on the top floor.
The thing Mrs Lulu Lamb
liked best was watching her
widescreen TV.

One of the things Nipper liked best was swinging on her TV aerial. "You little hooligan," she shouted. "Go home before I report you to the police."

"Oh, well," thought Nipper. It was
almost suppertime, anyway,
and his stomach was rumbling.

But it would be a long time
before Nipper saw his supper.
Those tiresome basement rats had
worked out a new plan to Get Nipper!
And Nipper walked right into the trap.

The lift doors slammed behind him.
Then, for the next half an hour,
those mean rats sent the lift up . . .

LIFT

. . . and down . . .

. . . and up . . .

. . . and down . . .

. . . until Nipper felt as if he'd turned into a yo-yo.

Poor Nipper was feeling sick,
but the rats didn't care.

They were nearly tripping over
their own tails laughing.

Finally the rats got bored – and hungry. They all went home for supper. They left the lift with Nipper inside – stuck on the top floor.

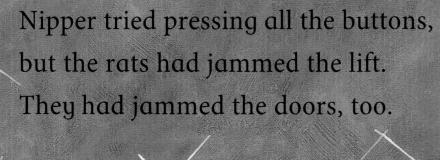

Nipper tried pressing all the buttons,
but the rats had jammed the lift.
They had jammed the doors, too.

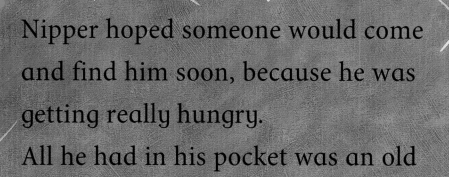

Nipper hoped someone would come
and find him soon, because he was
getting really hungry.
All he had in his pocket was an old
sticky Fishy Chew.

At that very moment Mrs McFee
was serving up Nipper's favourite
dish: mouse and kidney pie.
"Where is that boy?" she asked.

16

"Probably out with his no-good friends," said his brother, Monty. "Getting into more trouble," said Mimi and Fifi.

"We'll eat his share," they all agreed.

Meanwhile, Nipper tried yelling
at the top of his voice,
"Help! Is anybody there?"
But no one heard him.

Nipper even tried Morse Code.
He tapped – very loudly – on the
wall of the lift.
But sadly no one got Nipper's
message either.

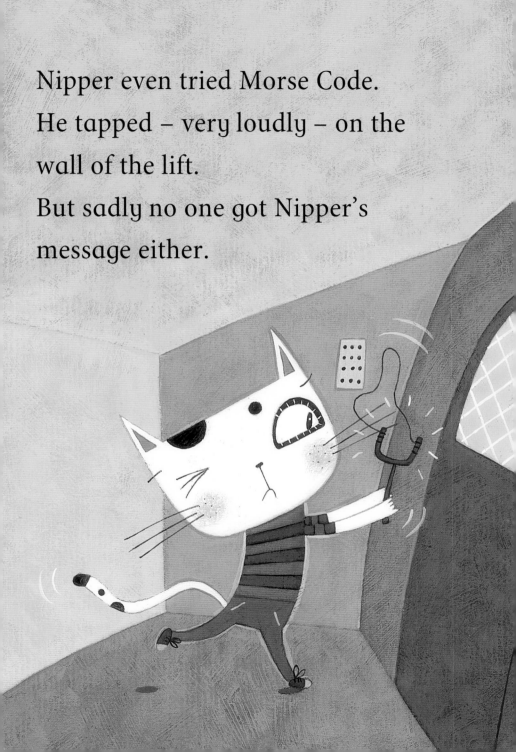

Not even Mrs Lulu Lamb heard
Nipper. She was watching TV.
It was a cowboy film with lots of

shooting and Red Indians yelling.
She had the volume turned up high
because she was a little bit deaf.

By now Nipper was hungry and bored! Nipper had the shiny new catapult and a pocket full of stones – but nothing to shoot at. Where was the fun in that?

In frustration Nipper rained a storm
of stones against the lift walls.

Clatter, bang!

Clatter, bang!

Clatter, bang!

Just then Mrs Lulu Lamb's film
ended. She heard a clattering
noise coming through the wall
of her flat.

When she went out to investigate,
she found . . .

Nipper McFee!

"It wasn't me. It was those rats!"
Nipper tried to convince her.
But Mrs Lulu Lamb wasn't
convinced.

She gave Nipper a real earwigging
before she let him go.

Because he came home so late,
Nipper got another telling off from
his mum.
Then he was sent to bed – with
no supper.

Nipper lay awake, listening to his
stomach rumbling. He had to find
a way to get even with those
rotten rodents.

Finally he came up with a plan.

The next day, Nipper got his revenge. As usual, the rats were only too happy to chase Nipper – all the way to the top of the building.

Come and get me!

Get Nipper!

But when they got there, Nipper's friends, Wil and Lil, had a little surprise waiting for the rats.

It was rubbish day.

The rats tumbled down the chute . . .

and straight into the rubbish truck.

Nipper and his friends cheered as
the rubbish was driven away.
It was about time those rats learned
not to mess with Nipper!

ROSE IMPEY ✳ MELANIE WILLIAMSON

All priced at £4.99

Orchard Books are available from all good bookshops,
or can be ordered from our website: www.orchardbooks.co.uk,
or telephone 01235 827702, or fax 01235 827703.

Prices and availability are subject to change.